A small seed in the muddle,
A sprout coming up for air,
A blooming . . .

That's How It Is When We Draw

Poems and Pictures by
Ruth Lercher Bornstein

Clarion Books ✳ New York

Clarion Books
a Houghton Mifflin Company imprint
215 Park Avenue South, New York, NY 10003
Text and illustrations copyright © 1997 by Ruth Lercher Bornstein

The illustrations for this book were executed in pencil and watercolor on Arches watercolor paper.
The text is set in 24/27-point Blueprint bold.

For information about this and other Houghton Mifflin trade and reference books
and multimedia products, visit The Bookstore at Houghton Mifflin
on the World Wide Web at (http://www.hmco.com/trade/).

Printed in Singapore

Library of Congress Cataloging-in-Publication Data

Bornstein, Ruth.
That's how it is when we draw / written and illustrated by Ruth Bornstein.
p.   cm
Summary: A young girl creates all kinds of wonderful pictures and expresses her feelings when she draws.
ISBN: 0-395-82509-1
[1. Artists—Fiction. 2. Imagination—Fiction.] I. Title.
PZ7.B64848Th
[E]—dc21   1997   96-49646
CIP
AC

TWP 10 9 8 7 6 5 4 3 2 1

This book is dedicated to
every growing and surprising thing

—R.L.B.

You do?
You want to come over?

But I need to be alone
In a quiet place today
And draw.

You do?
You want to draw too?

Okay!
I guess when we draw
We can be alone together.

7

WITH JUST ONE PENCIL

I can make monster creatures,
Make them bump each other,
Poke and shove each other,
Fill my paper with their roars.
Except in one corner.

They don't see the tiny ladybug on a tree.
They don't know yet that the ladybug
Is going to help them make up with each other,
Is going to tame them.

Is going to invite them
To her birthday picnic.

First eyes,
Then the nose.
Lips are hard.
She looks sad,
Poor thing.
I smile down at her,
Open her lips,
Give her teeth.
Now she's glad.
She smiles back at me.
I think I know that face.
Come see!
I've just made a picture
Of me!

Sometimes
I don't know what
My hand will draw and it
Surprises me. Sometimes it's the
Strangest thing: my
Own hand.

Then, out of nowhere,
A bug lands on my paper,
A bug with beautiful wings.

It seems to look at me,
It waves an arm—or a leg—at me.

And I hold very still,
I want it to stay,
But it waves goodbye,
It flies away.

I'm sad . . . and then
On my paper, I draw it.

The bug with beautiful wings
Is mine.

But sometimes . . .
There are bad times,

And I go away under the table,
And scribble everyone away.

Until the paper rips to pieces,
Until I punch it and scrunch it,
Until it's a tighter ball than anyone,

Until I throw everyone
Away.

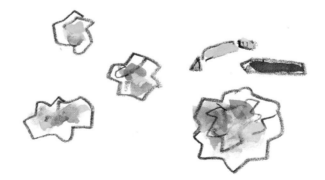

And then
Another time . . .

A rainbow!

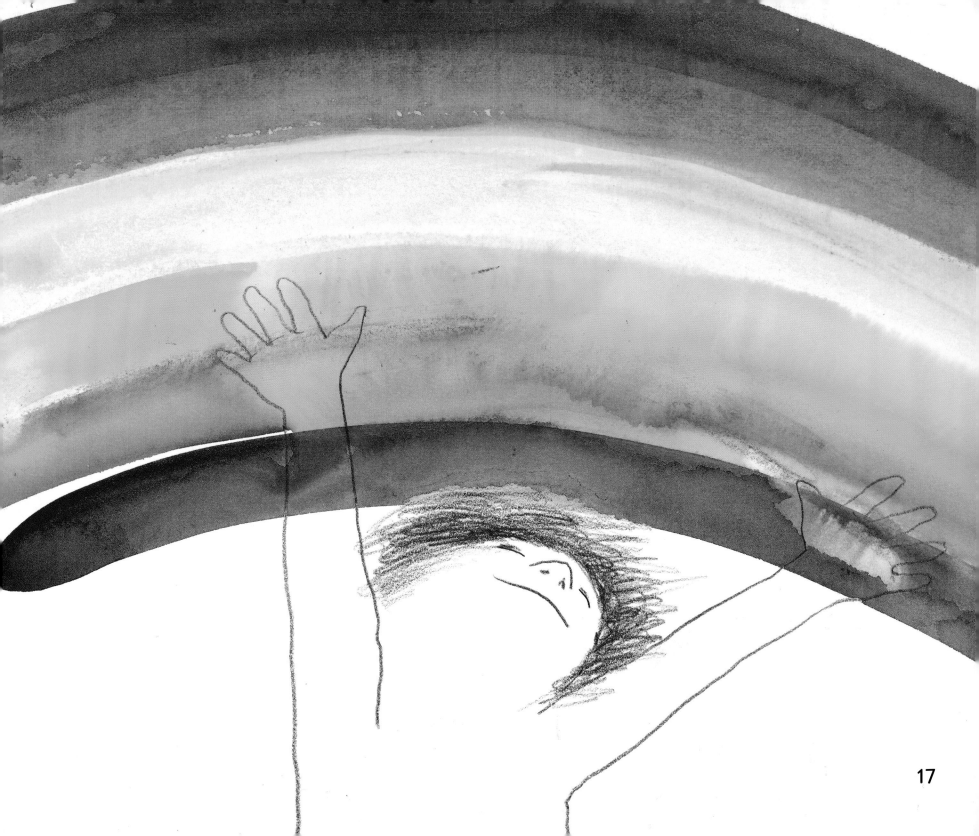

Newspaper,
Wrapping paper,
Brown paper bags.

Cereal box insides,
Envelope back sides,
Junk mail other sides,

DRAWING STUFF

18

I collect it all.

Because . . .
An important thing about drawing
Is . . .
Having lots of stuff to draw on!

Red paint, yellow, and blue,
With brush, paper, and water
Make orange, purple, and green,
Make lots of colors.

Splashing together,
Mixing,
Being friendly,
They make brown.

It's a nice brown.
I like it!
I'm going to make a man.

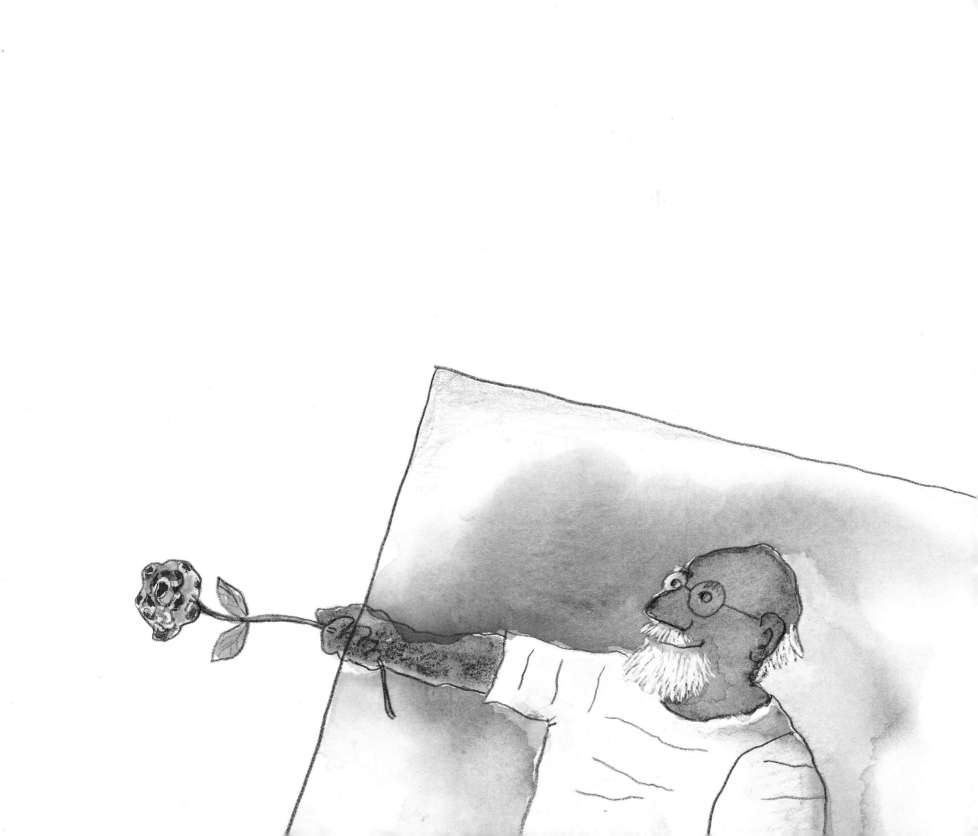

"You do not know our ways,"
They say,
"But here we are,
The forest people,
Showing ourselves to you at last,
Right here
In your own drawing."

And here is a bird above me,
Here is the ground below.
The ground feels good
As if it knows me,
As if the bird knows me,
And the sky.
As if they're all saying to me,
"You're here in the world,
And we know it."

WARNING!

You can walk out the door
On my wide red road.
You can jump on my orange river
Down the block.
But when you go around the corner,
Be careful . . .

Don't step on the whales
In my deep, green sea.

Pushing up from somewhere,
Bursting out from under,
Squiggles and doodles,
Shapes and colors.

Flowers stretching out,
People, and cats.
Elephants coming up,
Antelopes, and cows.

Fish, growing to the corners,
Frogs, blooming past the edges . . .

That's how it is when we draw.